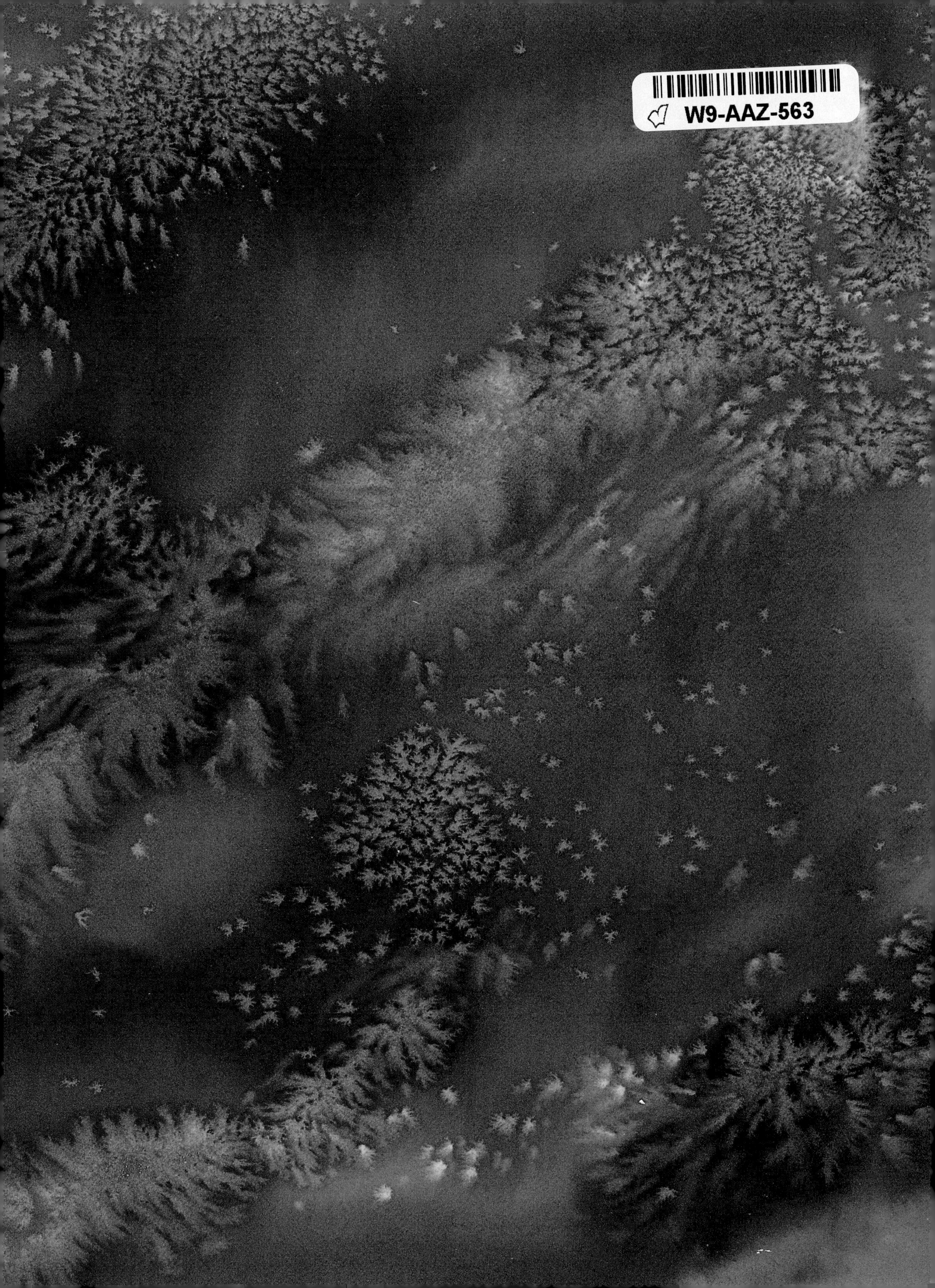

For Smitty, with love

M.W.

For my mother
for helping Ginny and me
create our first snowhorses,
and for giving me my
first real horse

C.W.M.

The illustrations in this book were rendered in watercolor. Typeset in Goudy Bold.
Book design by Laura Jane Coats. Printed in Singapore.
Library of Congress Cataloging-in-Publication Data
McGeorge, Constance W.
Snow Riders / by Constance W. McGeorge; illustrated by Mary Whyte.
32 p. 21.59 x 27.94 cm.
Summary: Matthew and his sister Molly build snowhorses that come to life
when they take a ride in the moonlight.
ISBN 0-8118-0873-4
[1. Brothers and sisters — Fiction. 2. Snow — Fiction. 3. Horses — Fiction.]
I. Whyte, Mary, ill. II. Title.
PZ7.M478467Sn 1995 [E] — dc20 94-47214 CIP AC
Distributed in Canada by Raincoast Books
8680 Cambie Street, Vancouver, British Columbia V6P 6M9
10 9 8 7 6 5 4 3 2 1
Chronicle Books
275 Fifth Street, San Francisco, California 94103

12/95
MERRY CHRISTMAS, KATIE!!
Maybe you all can try to make a "snow horse" this year – it sounds like it would be lots of fun!
Love,
Aunt Geralyn

SNOW RIDERS

Donated to Assumption School 11/2000

by

CONSTANCE W. MCGEORGE

illustrated by

MARY WHYTE

Chronicle Books • San Francisco

It was almost bedtime. Matthew was already in his pajamas. His sister Molly was busy drawing.

"It's snowing!" Matthew exclaimed.

"Maybe we'll get to stay home from school tomorrow," said Molly.

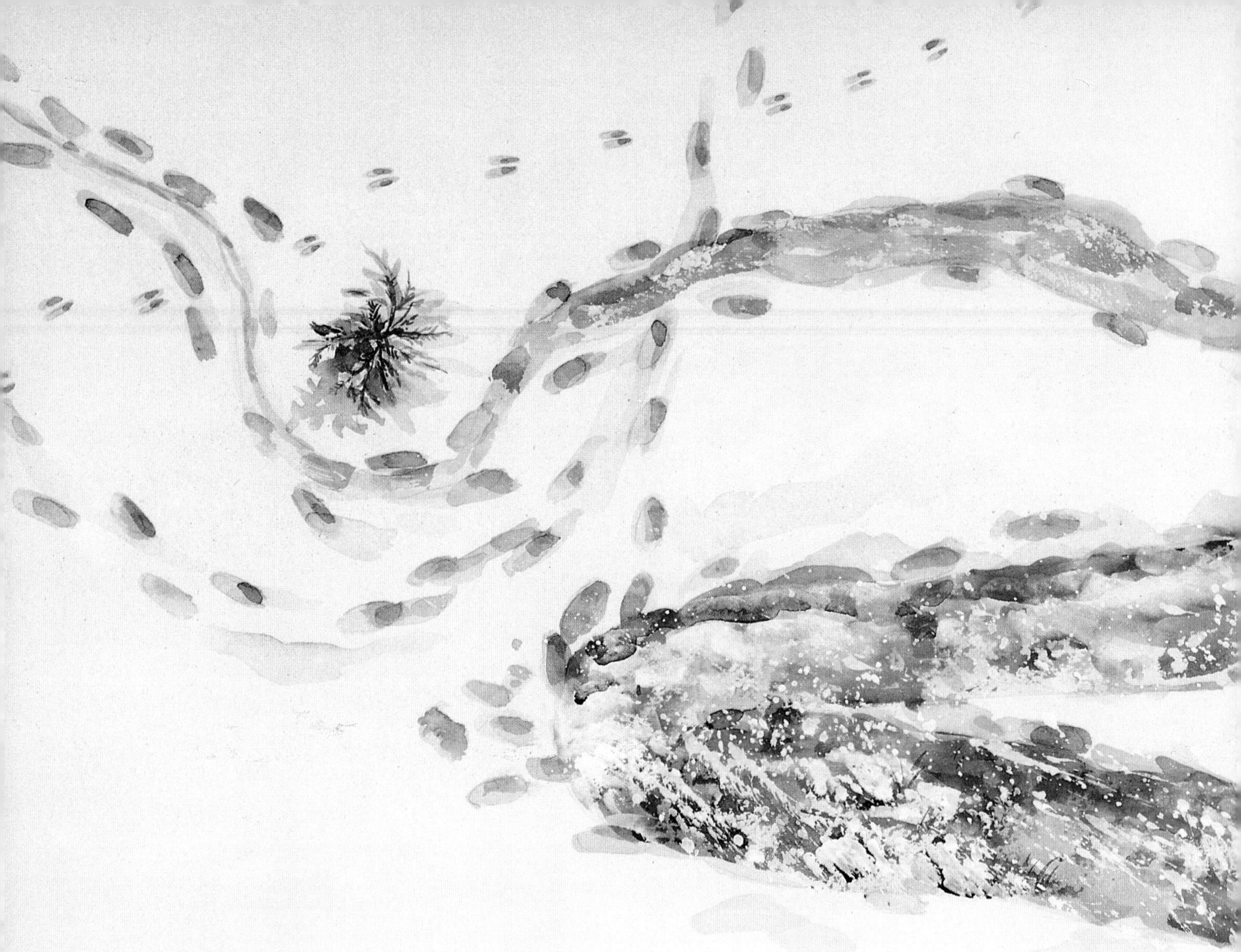

By morning, the neighborhood was buried in white. School was canceled. Molly and Matthew could hardly wait to go outside!

Molly rushed out into the yard and started rolling a snowball. Matthew helped her, and together they pushed the snowball through the deep snow. When it was finally big enough, they started to make another.

Molly and Matthew finished the second snowball, and then a third. But instead of stacking them one on top of the other, they placed them side by side, and then they made three more.

All day long they worked. They packed and pounded handfuls of snow over, under, and between the big snowballs. Finally, their creations were complete — with eyes and ears and flowing manes and tails!

But the sun was going down fast. Before they knew it, Molly and Matthew were called inside for supper.

That night, Molly and Matthew stood at Molly's bedroom window. They gazed at the snowhorses shining brightly in the moonlight.

"Let's go," Molly whispered.

Crunch, crunch, they crept across the sparkling snow. Under the midnight moon, they climbed onto the cold, silent snowhorses. They held imaginary bridle reins and bounced up and down, pretending to ride.

Matthew kicked his heels into the side of his snowhorse. "Giddy-up!" he commanded.

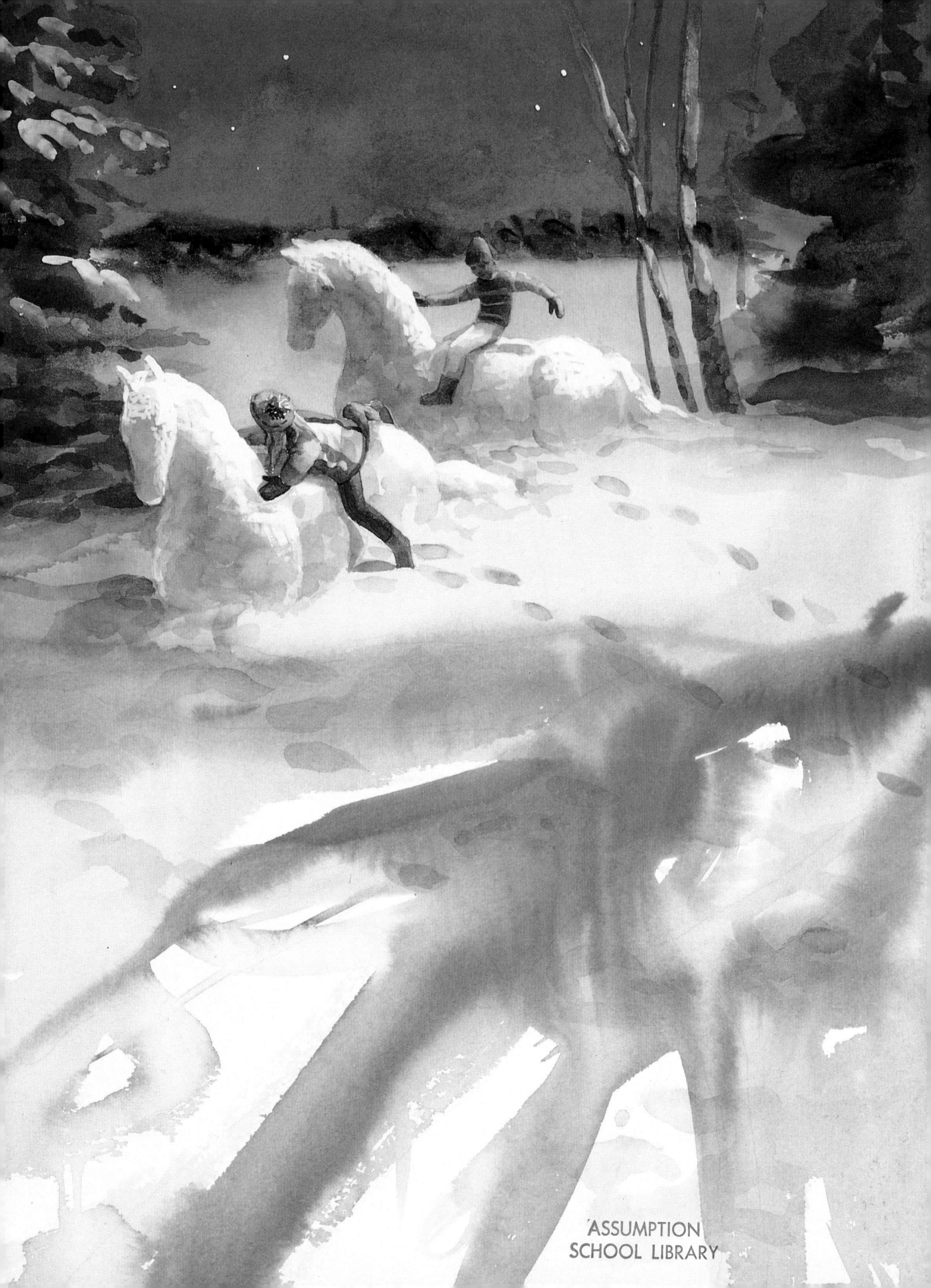

Suddenly, the snowhorse swung its head around!
It whinnied and flashed a bright shining eye.

Then Molly's horse shook its head and tail. Powerful long legs unfolded, and with a rumble, the giant horses heaved themselves upward.

The horses pranced in place and then cantered out of the yard. Molly and Matthew grabbed locks of mane and squeezed their legs tight against the horses' sides.

The horses splashed across an icy stream and through the woods into a wide open field.

Then the horses started to race! Ears back, necks flat, they charged into a full gallop, tearing across the field at lightning speed.

Molly and Matthew held on tight. Their faces tingled from the icy wind and the flying snow.

Suddenly, Molly saw something at the end of the field. It was a fence! Molly held her breath as her horse perked his ears and collected his stride. Then her horse tucked up his knees and jumped the fence clean.

"Lean forward," Molly shouted back at Matthew, "and don't look down!"

Matthew leaned forward, his face into the wind. His horse jumped high into the air and cleared the fence.

The horses galloped on. They crossed another open field and headed up a steep hill.

Finally, the horses slowed down to rest. Molly and Matthew looked out over the valley and up at the starry sky. They listened for a long time to the quiet of the night. The familiar sound of a train whistle drifted up the hill. "Is that the morning train?" asked Matthew.

The horses turned and started walking down the hill. The moon lit the way to Molly and Matthew's front yard. The horses were warm and steam rose from their backs. They stood very still, with their heads held high, as their riders slid off. Molly and Matthew lingered a moment, stroking and patting the horses. Then they turned away and slipped quietly back into the house.

As the moon disappeared
behind a cloud, Molly
and Matthew tiptoed up
to their rooms and soon
they were fast asleep.